JACKIE ROBINSON

By Lucia Raatma

WORLD ALMANAC® LIBRARY

Please visit our web site at: www.worldalmanaclibrary.com
For a free color catalog describing World Almanac® Library's
list of high-quality books and multimedia programs,
call 1-800-848-2928 or fax your request to (414) 332-3567.

Library of Congress Cataloging-in-Publication Data

Raatma, Lucia.
    Jackie Robinson / by Lucia Raatma.
      p. cm. — (Trailblazers of the modern world)
    Includes bibliographical references and index.
    Summary: Presents the life and career of the baseball legend who became the first African American to play in the major leagues.
    ISBN 0-8368-5072-6 (lib. bdg.)
    ISBN 0-8368-5232-X (softcover)
    1. Robinson, Jackie, 1919-1972—Juvenile literature. 2. Baseball players—United States—Biography—Juvenile literature. 3. African American baseball players—Biography—Juvenile literature. [1. Robinson, Jackie, 1919-1972. 2. Baseball players. 3. African Americans—Biography.] I. Title. II. Series.
    GV865.R6R323   2002
    796.357'092—dc21
    [B]   2001045628

This North American edition first published in 2002 by
World Almanac® Library
330 West Olive Street, Suite 100
Milwaukee, WI 53212 USA

This U.S. edition © 2002 by World Almanac® Library.

An Editorial Directions book
Editor: Pam Rosenberg
Designer and page production: Ox and Company
Photo researcher: Dawn Friedman
Indexer: Tim Griffin
World Almanac® Library art direction: Tammy Gruenewald
World Almanac® Library production: Susan Ashley and Jessica L. Yanke

Photo credits: AP/Wide World Photos, cover; National Baseball Hall of Fame Library, Cooperstown, NY/Barney Steil, 4; Corbis, 5; Hulton Archive, 6, 7; Corbis, 8, 9 top; Hulton Archive, 9 bottom; Corbis, 11, 12, 13, 15; Hulton Archive, 16, 17; Corbis, 18, 19, 20; AP/Wide World Photos, 21; Corbis, 22 top, 22 bottom; Hulton Archive, 23, 25; Corbis, 26 top; National Baseball Hall of Fame Library, Cooperstown, NY/Brooklyn Public Library Brooklyn Collection, 26 bottom; AP/Wide World Photos, 27; Hulton Archive, 29, 30, 31 top, 31 bottom, 33; AP/Wide World Photos, 34; Hulton Archive 35; AP/Wide World Photos, 36, 37, 38 top; Corbis, 38 middle, 38 bottom; AP/Wide World Photos, 39; Hulton Archive, 40; AP/Wide World Photos, 41, 42, 43.

Printed in the United States of America

1 2 3 4 5 6 7 8 9 06 05 04 03 02

TABLE of CONTENTS

Words that appear in the glossary are printed in **boldface**
type the first time they occur in the text.

CHAPTER 1

BREAKING THE COLOR LINE

On April 15, 1947, something remarkable happened. Jackie Robinson, wearing his now-famous number 42 jersey, played his first baseball game as a Brooklyn Dodger. His performance was not so remarkable, though. In fact, at his first appearance at the plate, he was thrown out at first base, and he didn't have a hit all day. He did field well, however, and he played first base with an efficiency that led the Dodgers to a 5–3 win over the Boston Braves. What made Robinson's performance so special was one thing: he was the first black American to play in **major league baseball**.

On April 15, 1947, Jackie Robinson made history by breaking the color line in major league baseball.

RACIAL INEQUALITY

In the 1940s, major league baseball in the United States was a sport for white men. Since the late 1800s, black players participated in the Negro Leagues, while the major leagues were for white players, and unfortunately, racial **discrimination** was not limited to the baseball diamond.

For decades, black Americans were not given the same rights as white Americans. Even though blacks had been given the right to vote by the Fifteenth Amendment in 1870, and they had been promised equal treatment by the Fourteenth Amendment in 1868, many inequalities still existed. Laws in the northern United States treated

African-Americans more fairly than those in the South did, but racism was still an issue. Most black Americans did not have the same job opportunities as whites, and they were often the victims of small-minded **racists**. Meanwhile, laws in the South forced African-Americans to sit in separate areas in restaurants, public buses, stadiums, and waiting rooms. They even had to drink from separate water fountains. This **segregation** led many people to fight for **civil rights** and to change the system, but change was slow in coming.

For many years, black Americans faced segregation in public places.

ON AND OFF THE PLAYING FIELD

Today, Robinson is remembered for breaking the color line in baseball as well as for being one of baseball's most exciting players. A talented athlete, he led the national league in stolen bases in 1947 and 1949, and he was named the 1947 **Rookie** of the Year. He was a determined player who always knew how to come through for his team, and along the way, he earned the respect of his teammates and the admiration of many fans.

When his days as a player were over, Robinson went on to work for social equality in other areas as well. At times, his ideas were considered controversial, and some people resented his outspoken nature, but Robinson felt that it was his duty to speak out against racism and injustice. Sometimes he did not agree with other black leaders in the civil rights movement, and sometimes he said things he later regretted.

Through it all, Robinson remained true to himself, and he strove to make the United States a better place for people of all races, both on and off the playing field.

CHAPTER 2

THE YOUNG ATHLETE

The early part of Jackie Robinson's life was marked by challenges and difficulties. These hardships became a part of him and helped him become the man we now remember.

Jack Roosevelt Robinson was born on January 31, 1919, in Cairo, Gerogia. His parents were Mallie and Jerry Robinson, and he was the youngest of their five children. His brothers were Edgar, Frank, and Mack, and his sister was Willa Mae. Jackie's grandfather had been a slave in the South, and his father worked as a **sharecropper** on a plantation near Cairo. Sharecroppers had better lives than the slaves had, but they still made very little money. One day, when Jackie was about six months old, Jerry Robinson left in search of better work, but he never came back. Jerry and Mallie's marriage had been strained for some time, but the family never quite understood what drove him away. At one point, they heard that he headed to Florida with another man's wife. Jackie Robinson grew up with no memory of his father, but he was told a few stories about him by his siblings—mostly negative ones. Many years later, the family received a telegram informing them of Jerry's death.

Sharecroppers worked long, hard days for very little pay.

With her husband gone, Mallie Robinson suddenly found herself as the sole provider for five children. She worried about the life her children would have in rural Georgia, so in 1920, she moved the family to California. Her half-brother lived there, and he encouraged Mallie to move to Pasadena. At that time, most of the residents of this Los Angeles suburb were white, but Mallie was determined to give her children the best she could.

Jackie Robinson (second from left) with his mother and siblings in the 1920s

ON PEPPER STREET

The Robinson family eventually settled into a house on Pepper Street. Many other residents of the neighborhood were not happy to see the Robinsons move in. In fact, they signed a **petition** to try to force the family to leave.

Although Pasadena was far from the **Deep South**, racial segregation still existed there in more subtle forms. Blacks and whites lived in different neighborhoods for the most part. The local pool, though open to both races in theory, allowed blacks to swim there only one day a week, while the local movie theater had its African-American patrons sit upstairs in the balcony.

The Robinsons were often taunted by other children who called them a wide range of racist names, but the Robinsons did not allow the insults from their neighbors to bother them too much. They turned to one another for strength, and they tried to take pride in themselves. Mallie worked very hard as a domestic servant and was

The Robinsons left the South for Pasadena, California, in 1920.

often not home, but Jackie and his siblings knew what was expected of them. She instilled a strong religious faith in her offspring, and she taught them to look out for one another.

Remembering Mallie

In his autobiography, *I Never Had It Made*, Jackie Robinson had this to say about his mother:

I remember, even as a small boy, having a lot of pride in my mother. I thought she must have some kind of magic to be able to do all the things she did, to work so hard and never complain and to make us all feel happy. We had our family squabbles and spats, but we were a well-knit unit. My pride in my mother was tempered with a sense of sadness that she had to bear most of our burdens. At a very early age I began to want to relieve her in any small way I could. I was happy whenever I had money to give her.

AT SCHOOL AND IN THE NEIGHBORHOOD

Mallie Robinson worked long hours to support her family, so Willa Mae was expected to help take care of Jackie. Before he was old enough to enroll in school, Jackie tagged along with Willa Mae. While she attended classes, he played in the school sandbox. It was a lonely time for him even though everyone at the school was very nice to him. He was happy when he was finally old enough to "graduate" from the sandbox and become a real student.

Jackie did not excel in the classroom, but he made a name for himself on the playing field. In

fact, all the Robinson boys were great athletes. Mack Robinson was a track-and-field star, and he represented the United States at the 1936 Olympic Games in Berlin, Germany. He earned a silver medal in the 200-meter

Mack Robinson (left) and Jesse Owens (second from right) at the 1936 Olympic track-and-field trials.

Jesse Owens

Jesse Owens was a talented African-American athlete who represented the United States in the 1936 Olympic Games. The competition that year was held in Germany, a country ruled by Adolf Hitler. Hitler, the leader of Germany's Nazi Party, believed that the white race was superior to all others, and he was sure his German athletes would show that.

Jesse Owens was certain he could prove Hitler wrong, and he didn't give in to the hatred that surrounded him. He triumphed in the track-and-field events and brought home four gold medals. By the time the Olympics ended that year, even the German fans were cheering for Owens.

dash, finishing second only to the amazing Jesse Owens. Owens won four gold medals that year.

Unfortunately, Jackie got involved with the wrong crowd. He and other boys stole items from stores, **vandalized** cars, and played tricks on people in the neighborhood. He was often in trouble with the police and could easily have become a **juvenile delinquent**. Luckily, two men stepped into Jackie's life and helped him. A mechanic named Carl Anderson became friends with Jackie and convinced him that these actions would hurt both him and his mother. Anderson explained that following the crowd was not something to be proud of. Meanwhile, Karl Downs, the family's minister, helped Jackie separate himself from this group of young men and turn his attention to church activities. Downs worked hard to pull young people into the church community, and Jackie benefited from the minister's attention and advice.

HIGH SCHOOL AND COLLEGE

At John Muir Technical High School, Jackie Robinson proved himself to be an asset to almost any team. He earned letters in four sports—football, basketball, baseball, and track—and he came to rely on the encouragement his brothers gave him.

After high school, Jackie enrolled at Pasadena Junior College. While a student there, he played on championship baseball, basketball, and football teams,

At UCLA, Robinson excelled in football as well as other sports.

and he continued to compete in track-and-field events as well. His success caught the eye of coaches from a number of universities, and he was offered several athletic scholarships for his final two years of college.

From those colleges that offered him scholarships, Jackie chose the University of California at Los Angeles (UCLA). There he again excelled in basketball, baseball, football, and track, becoming the first person at UCLA to letter in four sports. Jackie was the leading scorer on the basketball team, and he was was named a football All-American.

Without a doubt, he was a great athlete, but in the United States during the early 1940s, few positions were open to black men in professional sports. Jackie began to think about his future, and he wondered how he would make a living.

CHAPTER 3

ON HIS OWN

By the spring of 1941, Jackie Robinson had used up his years of **athletic eligibility**, so he could no longer play college sports. He had not finished all the courses needed for his degree, but he decided to leave UCLA nonetheless. Jackie wanted to help relieve the financial burden his mother had always been under, so he decided it was time to get a job and make money.

A welding class sponsored by the National Youth Administration, a group that provided a variety of programs for young people in need.

AFTER COLLEGE

Robinson would have loved to make a living as a professional athlete, but the sports world was not really open to African-Americans at that time. He was able to play football on a semi-professional team for a while, but he supported himself by serving as an assistant athletic director for the National Youth Administration, a group that provided athletic and educational programs to young people in need. Most of the youths the group helped came from poor backgrounds or single-parent families.

This position was one that Robinson enjoyed because it kept him involved in sports and enabled him to help young people as well. However, he did not stay with the organization for very long. In late 1941, the United States entered World War II (1939–1945), and in March 1942, Robinson was drafted into the U.S. Army.

SECOND LIEUTENANT ROBINSON

After Robinson completed his basic training at Fort Riley, Kansas, he hoped to enroll in Officers' Candidate School (OCS). He soon learned, however, that although he qualified for the school, he was not allowed to attend. For weeks, he and other black soldiers were kept out of the OCS program.

Help came from an unusual source: heavyweight champion boxer Joe Louis. By coincidence, Louis was also in the army and was transferred to Fort Riley where Robinson had the opportunity to speak with him. Louis was angry at the unequal treatment Robinson and the other African-Americans were receiving, and he took action. He called around and used his name to bring attention to the problem. Suddenly, political figures in Washington were pressuring the administration at Fort Riley, and the OCS opened its doors to Robinson and the other black American men. Robinson excelled at OCS, and in January 1943 he was made a second lieutenant, but Robinson's experiences with racism in the military were not over.

Famed boxer Joe Louis came to Robinson's aid when both men served in the U.S. Army.

A SEGREGATED ARMY

In many ways, the incident with OCS was only the beginning of Robinson's problems in the army. Because of his athletic skill and his

Army Baseball

In early 1943, Robinson decided to check out Fort Riley's baseball team. Pete Reiser, who later played with Robinson as a Dodger, happened to be a member of the army team. He remembered:

One day a Negro lieutenant came out for the ball team. An officer told him he couldn't play. "You'll have to play for the colored team," the officer said. That was a joke. There was no colored team. The lieutenant didn't say anything. He stood there for a while, watching us work out. Then he turned and walked away. I didn't know who he was then, but that was the first time I saw Jackie Robinson. I can still remember him walking away by himself.

college reputation, Robinson was asked to play on the army football team. He was happy to be back on the football field, but that happiness was short-lived. After practicing with the other players and preparing to take on both military and college teams, Robinson learned that some other teams refused to compete against black players. The army tried to downplay this problem, but Robinson was so furious that he quit the team. Later, he encountered similar problems with the baseball team.

Soon Robinson was transferred to Fort Hood, Texas, and there he excelled. In April 1944, he was made a platoon leader, which meant he led a group of men and made sure weapons and vehicles were carefully inspected. He also did well organizing the unit's athletic teams, and he was a key player on the baseball and softball teams. He impressed the unit leader, Colonel Paul Bates, who once explained, "Jackie Robinson gained pride and strength as a leader from our men. He got as much or more from them as he himself gave."

Unfortunately, this positive period in the army proved short. In July 1944, while riding in an army bus, he was instructed to move to a seat in the back. This was a common occurrence for black Americans in civilian life, which was governed by **Jim Crow laws** in the 1940s. It wasn't until the 1950s that black Americans were treated fairly on public buses—but the army had

Jim Crow Laws

Long before television and radio were popular, entertainment often came in the form of **vaudeville** and **minstrel** shows. Some of the performers in these shows (right) dressed in outlandish costumes, painted their faces black, and proceeded to make fun of African-Americans.

One such performer was Thomas Dartmouth "Daddy" Rice, who in 1828 created a blackface show called "Jump Jim Crow." This routine soon became known all over the country, and other performers imitated it. "Jim Crow," which had been a nickname for the blackbird, soon came to be a hateful term used for black Americans.

Years later, laws intended to segregate blacks from whites were implemented throughout the South. Blacks and whites were kept separate in schools and restaurants, waiting rooms and parks. Blacks had to sit in the back seats of buses, while whites sat in the front. In time, these unfair practices came to be known as Jim Crow laws.

supposedly abolished such unreasonable rules. When Robinson refused to move, the bus driver turned him over to the military police, who later claimed that Robinson was drunk, used profanity, and was disrespectful of them and of the officers who questioned him.

Robinson claimed that these charges were not true, but before long he was facing a **court-martial**.

Before the trial began, Robinson wrote a letter to Joe Louis, and members of the press were told that the young black lieutenant was being set up. An anonymous person contacted the National Association for the Advancement of Colored People (NAACP) and informed the group that the charges against Robinson were false. Soon the army began to realize that convicting Robinson of drunk and disorderly conduct would result in embarrassing the military. In the end, some of the charges were dropped, and the army failed to produce convincing witnesses at the trial. Robinson was acquitted, but he knew that his life in the army was over. He wrote a letter asking for a discharge, and he got his wish. The army leaders considered him to be a troublemaker, so they were happy to be rid of him. Citing that Robinson had a physical injury that prevented him from service, the army granted him an honorable discharge in November 1944. After two and a half years as a soldier, Jackie Robinson was a civilian again.

As a Kansas City Monarch in 1944

KANSAS CITY, HERE I COME

Before leaving the army, Robinson met Hilton Smith, a fellow soldier who had played baseball in the Negro Leagues. Smith told Robinson that there was decent money in black baseball, and he knew that his former team—the Kansas City Monarchs—was looking for players. Robinson contacted the Monarchs, and they responded quickly. He reported to Houston for spring training and began earning $400 a month, a sum he referred to as a "financial bonanza." Robinson was back in a baseball uniform, and his life would never be the same.

Life in the Negro Leagues

Players in the Negro Leagues were happy to play baseball, but they had to endure a hard lifestyle. They traveled in broken-down buses and often had to sleep in those buses when motels turned them away. When restaurants wouldn't serve them, they often ate cold food on the buses as well.

Many remarkable players in the Negro Leagues never gained the fame they might have had today.

Josh Gibson, a catcher for the Homestead Grays (above) and other teams, is considered the first and only player to hit a ball completely out of Yankee Stadium. He hit 75 home runs in 1931, 69 in 1934, 84 in 1936, and 962 over the course of his career.

Satchel Paige, who pitched for the Pittsburgh Crawfords among other teams, was an entertaining as well as a talented player. To show his confidence in his own ability, he used to send his entire outfield into the dugout when the best hitter from the opposing team came up to bat. Once Paige finally made it to the major leagues, legendary player Joe DiMaggio called him "the best and fastest player I've ever faced."

Cool Papa Bell was one of the most dangerous hitters and by far the fastest base runner in Negro Leagues history. His speed resulted in wild stories that just got more and more unbelievable: one told of Bell hitting a ground ball up the middle and being hit by that same ball while sliding into second.

In 1933, more than twenty thousand fans attended the Negro National League All-Star Game, and four years later, the Negro American League was formed. Though these teams never enjoyed the popularity of their white counterparts, they won the hearts of many fans, and they produced some memorable players—athletes who deserved more fame and attention than they ever received.

THE EXPERIMENT

CHAPTER 4

Jackie Robinson did his best for the Kansas City Monarchs, but he was discouraged. He knew that black baseball players had a limited future, and he didn't know what he should do next. He continued to help his mother financially, so he needed to make more money. Also, he wanted to marry Rachel Isum, a young woman he had been dating since his days at UCLA. Little did he know that his future lay in the hands of a man named Branch Rickey.

Branch Rickey was the general manager for the Brooklyn Dodgers when he decided the time was right to bring African-Americans into major league baseball.

MEETING BRANCH RICKEY

When Robinson first met Branch Rickey, Rickey was president of the Brooklyn Dodgers baseball organization. However, Rickey had been playing a role in baseball for many years. He had coached college teams and held executive positions for major league teams. Along the way, he always fought for the rights of black athletes, but his efforts were not successful.

One incident in particular stuck with him over the years. When he was a coach for Ohio Wesleyan University, a hotel manger had refused admittance to Charley Thomas, the team's African-American first baseman. Rickey was furious and threatened to move the entire team to another hotel, but finally the hotel management gave in and allowed Thomas to sleep on

Baseball in Cuba

It is said that Cubans have a passion for baseball, and in fact, the Cuban love of the sport has a rich history. Cuba's first organized league play began in 1878 (just two years after the birth of the U.S. National League and twenty-two years before the birth of the American League), and from the beginning it offered a racial equality that the U.S. leagues did not. During the sixty years when black baseball players were banned from U.S. major leagues, blacks and whites competed freely in Cuba. Many of the greatest interracial games of the era took place in Havana, rather than in New York's Yankee Stadium, and many of the black stars of the U.S. Negro Leagues, who trained in Cuba during the off-season, were happy to call the island their home away from home.

a cot in Rickey's room. That night, Rickey watched Thomas cry and scratch at his hands, saying that he wished they were white. This incident and others proved to Rickey that the unfairness had to end. By the time he was in charge of the Brooklyn Dodgers, he was ready to bring about change.

Branch Rickey had followed Robinson's career, and he knew what a good player the young man was. Rickey also had investigated Robinson's outspoken nature regarding the treatment of blacks in the army. He wanted to bring African-American players into major league baseball, but he knew he had to choose the first player very carefully. The person would have to be a great athlete, but he would also need to be brave and confident, as well as willing to stand up to all the controversy that was bound to brew. Among the Negro League players he considered were Satchel Paige, a brilliant player who finally reached the majors in 1948, and Josh Gibson, a player whose career was nearly over by the mid-1940s. Rickey searched throughout the United States and Cuba for the right person. After many months, he thought Robinson might be the man he was looking for.

Satchel Paige was a brilliant pitcher who played in the Negro Leagues before Robinson broke the color line.

Catcher Josh Gibson was reaching the end of his career by the time African-American players joined the major leagues.

In August 1945, Rickey sent a **scout** to talk to Robinson, with the story that the Brooklyn Brown Dodgers, a Negro team, was looking for new players. Robinson listened to the scout and agreed to meet with Rickey, but he had no idea what was really in store.

Once in Branch Rickey's office, Robinson was stunned to find out the real plans— what Rickey came to call the "noble experiment." Rickey explained that he believed baseball was ready for **integrated** teams, and he wanted Robinson to join his organization. First Robinson was to join the Montreal Royals, a **farm team** for the Brooklyn Dodgers. Then, when the time was right, he was to move up and officially play for the Dodgers. The biggest catch, however, was that Rickey wanted Robinson to keep his temper under control. He was never to react to taunts and jeering from the crowds. No matter what happened, he was never to fight back—not even if another player started a brawl.

Rickey said, "I think you can play in the major leagues. How do you feel about it?"

In *I Never Had It Made*, Robinson remembered his emotions. "My reactions seemed like some kind of weird mixture churning in a blender. I was thrilled, scared, and excited. I was incredulous. Most of all, I was speechless."

When Robinson was finally able to speak, he accepted the challenge. He knew that what lay ahead of him would not be easy. The experiment had begun.

TAKING BIG STEPS

Robinson agreed to a contract that stipulated a $3,500 signing bonus and a salary of $600 a month. At first, he kept his plans a secret from everyone except his mother and Rachel, to whom he was then engaged. For the next two months, Rickey and his organization set their plan in motion.

In October 1945, the world learned of Robinson's contract and Rickey's experiment. Many reporters said that Robinson would never make it as a major league player, and others worried that the Negro Leagues would fail if blacks could join the majors. The Kansas City Monarchs even threatened to sue the Royals since Robinson was under contract with the Monarchs, but eventually they backed down.

In February 1946, Jackie Robinson and Rachel Isum were married. Presiding at the ceremony was Robinson's mentor from the old neighborhood, Reverend Karl Downs. A few weeks later, Robinson reported for spring training.

Newlyweds Jackie and Rachel Robinson in February 1946

AS A MONTREAL ROYAL

Branch Rickey had chosen a man named Clay Hopper to manage the Montreal Royals. When he heard about Robinson being added to his team, Hopper begged Rickey to change his mind. He had grown up in the Deep

By the time Robinson became a Dodger, Royals manager Clay Hopper (left) had warmed up to the idea of African-American players in the major leagues.

Robinson crossing home plate after hitting a three-run home run on opening day for the Montreal Royals in 1946

South, and his family owned a large southern plantation. However, Rickey knew that Hopper was smart about baseball, and he was sure the manager and Robinson would work together just fine.

Robinson had a hard time in spring training. He initially played shortstop, but playing this position was very hard on his right arm. Soon his arm was so sore that he couldn't lift it, so Rickey moved him to second base, where a strong throw was not as crucial. In addition to his aching arm, Robinson had trouble with the **bigotry** he was facing. Nevertheless, he gave it his best, and by opening day, he was ready.

On April 18, 1946, Jackie Robinson played his first minor league game as a Montreal Royal. He was nervous about the big crowd in New Jersey that had come to see him perform, and at his first at-bat he hit a ground ball and was called out at first base.

When he came to bat the second time, two other

players were already on base. Robinson took a deep breath and a big right-handed swing. With a pop, the ball sailed long and out of the park—for a three-run home run. The Royals went on to beat the Jersey City Giants by a score of 14–1 that day. Robinson remembered, "When the game ended, I had four hits: a home run and three singles, and I had stolen two bases. I knew what it was that day to hear the ear-shattering roar of the crowd and know it was for me. I began to really believe one of Mr. Rickey's predictions. Color didn't matter to fans if the black man was [the] winner."

In the months to come, Robinson had many positive moments but also many negative ones. Fans screamed at him, and they called out racist comments. Other players tried to injure him, and he even felt resentment from some of his own teammates. However, he remembered his promise to Branch Rickey, and he showed the courage not to fight back.

One real joy for Jackie and Rachel was living in Montreal. The people of that Canadian city were warm and inviting. The Montreal fans cheered for Robinson and offered their undying support for their minor league team.

The city of Montreal was a warm and welcoming place for the Robinsons.

A Not-So-Sure Thing

William Brashler, writing in *The Story of Negro League Baseball*, described Jackie Robinson's challenge in this way:

Jackie Robinson.

Some people called him baseball's "great experiment." To Jackie Roosevelt Robinson, however, it was a chance. He was a black man in a white man's league. He was a ballplayer, and for him that was not an experiment, but a sure thing.

Except that in 1946, with millions—many of whom desperately wanted him to fail—watching his every move, nothing was a sure thing. He had to show proof of his ability. He had to represent his race. He had to match the talent of all those great Negro league players who never had a chance.

Few men or women, in or out of baseball, have ever had so much riding on their shoulders.

THE LITTLE WORLD SERIES

The minor league season culminated in a seven-game Little World Series between the **pennant** winners of the two leagues. The Royals, champions of the International League, faced the Louisville Colonels, champions of the American Association. During the first three games in Louisville, the fans let their disapproval of Robinson be known. One spectator yelled, "Hey, black boy, go back to Canada—and stay," while others called out many equally offensive racial **slurs**. Robinson found himself in a hitting slump, and the angry crowds only made it worse.

The Royals lost two of those first three games and returned to Montreal to play the final four. There the Canadian fans booed the Louisville players. They had heard about how the Montreal team had been treated in Louisville, and they were furious. The fans' loyalty—even though it was rather vengeful—cheered the Royals on. The team won the next three games and went on to win the championship. Robinson overcame his slump, performed well in the rest of the series, and scored the winning run in the final game. As Robinson left the stadium after the Royals' victory, he was mobbed by the grateful hometown fans. Suddenly, the outcast had become a hero.

MOVING UP

The following year, the Montreal Royals and the Brooklyn Dodgers held their spring training in Havana, Cuba. Branch Rickey hoped that Cuba, where blacks and whites were freely integrated, would provide the perfect backdrop for the next step in his experiment. By that time, the Royals had signed three more black players: Roy Partlow, Roy Campanella, and Don Newcombe. Rickey hoped that by adding these players to the Royals—and by having the Royals and Dodgers in spring training together—the Dodger players would become more accepting of African-Americans. Unfortunately, the plan did not work. Some Dodgers— including pitcher Kirby Higbe, catcher Bobby Bragan, second baseman Eddie Stanky, and pitcher Dixie Walker—even signed a petition saying they would not play if Robinson was moved to their team. Rickey threatened to kick them all off the team, however, and they backed down.

In addition to the racial pressure Robinson was under, there was also some confusion about what position he was to play. Rickey saw that the Dodger team had a fine shortstop in Pee Wee Reese, and second base was ably covered as well, but they were weak at third base and first base. Third base was a bad choice for Robinson because of his arm, so that left first base— a position in which Robinson felt awkward. In spite of that awkwardness, Rickey encouraged Robinson to play his very best when the Royals competed against the Dodgers in **exhibition games**. Robinson accepted the challenge and played spectacular baseball, but even that did not impress the Dodger players.

Rickey then asked Dodger manager Leo Durocher to tell the sports reporters that his team would have a shot at the pennant if Robinson played for them. He thought

Robinson taking the time to sign autographs for the enthusiastic fans in Havana, Cuba

Leo Durocher (left) was a supporter of Robinson's, but the Dodgers manager was suspended from baseball before he could further the young player's cause.

Ebbets Field, the stadium where the Dodgers played in Brooklyn, New York

such a quote would result in support from the Dodger fans, but before Durocher could make the statement, he was suspended from baseball. Baseball commissioner A. B. "Happy" Chandler, who was vocally against integrated baseball, claimed to have received information that Durocher was associating with known gamblers.

The allegation and the resulting suspension resulted in a public uproar, but Rickey knew he had another story that would knock the Durocher news off the front page. On April 9, 1947, on the morning of an exhibition game, Rickey handed reporters a one-line announcement: "Brooklyn announces the purchase of the contract of Jack Roosevelt Robinson from Montreal." It wasn't long before the news traveled all over the world.

THE FIRST GAME

Less than a week after Branch Rickey's announcement, Jackie Robinson donned his number 42 uniform and played in his first major league game. The day was April 15, 1947, and the place was Ebbets Field in Brooklyn, New York. It would be great to say that Robinson played a remarkable game, stealing bases and scoring runs, but that isn't the way it worked out. As it happened, Robinson was in another slump. In his four appearances at bat, he failed to reach base even once. Obviously, he was disappointed and maybe even embarrassed, but even though the day had not been perfect, something very big had happened. The color barrier had been broken.

AS A BROOKLYN DODGER

CHAPTER 5

In the days that followed Robinson's **debut** as a Dodger, he continued to play poorly. He began to doubt himself and Rickey's decision to sign him. However, both Rickey and manager Burt Shotton, who had replaced Durocher, were patient and encouraging. They knew the pressure Robinson was under, and they were sure the slump would end.

FACING THE PHILLIES

Early in that 1947 season, the Philadelphia Phillies came to Ebbets Field for three games against the Dodgers, and Jackie Robinson faced some of the worst abuse ever. When he approached the plate in the first

Robinson with (from left to right) John Jorgensen, Pee Wee Reese, and Ed Stanky—players who eventually became loyal teammates

Turning the Other Cheek

In *I Never Had It Made*, Robinson talked about that first game against the Philadelphia Phillies. It could have marked the end of his career, but it proved instead to be a turning point.

I have to admit that this day of all the unpleasant days in my life, brought me nearer to cracking up than I ever had been. Perhaps I should have become inured to this kind of garbage, but I was in New York City and unprepared to face the kind of barbarism from a northern team that I had come to associate with the Deep South. . . . I felt tortured and I tried just to play ball and ignore the insults. But it was really getting to me. What did the Phillies want from me? What, indeed, did Mr. Rickey expect of me? I was, after all, a human being. What was I doing here turning the other cheek as though I weren't a man? . . . How could I have thought that barriers would fall, that, indeed, my talent could triumph over bigotry?

inning, the Philadelphia players—egged on by their manager, Ben Chapman—called out a flurry of insults. "They're waiting for you in the jungles, black boy!" one player yelled. "We don't want you here," another shouted. Racist names flew out of the dugout, and Robinson couldn't believe his ears.

Robinson almost quit baseball that day. It was hard for him to keep his cool and not yell back at the racist players he faced. That April afternoon, he'd nearly had enough, but he dug down and just tried to play his best baseball. In the end, the Dodgers won that game, but the Phillies did not give up in their abuse.

During the next two games, the insults continued and were eventually directed at all of the Brooklyn players. The Phillies taunted Robinson and his teammates, but Robinson—remembering his promise to Branch Rickey—remained silent. Finally, Eddie Stanky, who had initially opposed Robinson's presence on the Dodgers team, could take no more. He hollered, "You yellow-bellied cowards, why don't you pick on somebody who can answer back!" In the end, Philadelphia's attempt to humiliate the Dodger team only brought the players together. Rickey was thrilled by the team unity, and he even publicly thanked Chapman for helping bring it about.

A MEMBER OF THE TEAM

The series against Philadelphia did in fact bring the Dodgers team together, and Robinson was accepted as part of the group. He and shortstop Pee Wee Reese, a player who hailed from the Deep South, had an important relationship on the field. Their shortstop and first base positions resulted in a number of fine double plays. This teamwork led to a connection between the two men, which was heightened during a game in Boston against the Braves. When fans heckled Reese, asking how he could play baseball with a black man, Reese's reaction was simply to walk over to first base, talk to Robinson for a moment, and put his arm around Robinson's shoulder. This incident solidified their friendship, and over the years, Robinson became friends with other teammates as well.

Spectacular shortstop Pee Wee Reese was a friend to Jackie Robinson.

Some teams in the major leagues were not so accepting, however. The St. Louis Cardinals players even threatened to strike if Robinson continued to play, but National League president Ford Frick told them in no uncertain terms that they would be suspended from baseball if they proceeded with their plan. Suddenly, both the National League and Robinson's team were behind him, and that support did wonders for his game.

SHOWING HIS STUFF

In the months that followed, Jackie Robinson led his team in excellence. He was at the top of the league in bases stolen and runs scored, but what was most exciting was the flair with which he played. He didn't just

Joe DiMaggio was one of the big-name players on the New York Yankees team that beat the Dodgers in the 1947 World Series.

score; in Chicago he once scored all the way from first base on a bunt. He didn't just steal a base; in Pittsburgh that year he stole home, something he would do again in his career.

Suddenly African-Americans became huge baseball fans. They came out to watch Robinson play, and they saw his success as a ray of hope. With every ball he hit, with every run he scored, black Americans saw possibilities. They saw that maybe things could get better, both in baseball and in everyday life.

As Robinson's rookie season came to an end, the Brooklyn Dodgers won the National League pennant and went on to face the American League's New York Yankees in the World Series. The Yankees—led by baseball greats Yogi Berra, Joe DiMaggio, and Phil Rizzuto—won the series, four games to three, but the Dodgers had much to be proud of. For his part, Jackie Robinson had reasons to be pleased as well. He finished with a .297 batting average, and he led the league in bases stolen (29). It had been a tough season for him, but an important one, and as it ended the young man was named Rookie of the Year.

The next year, Robinson started off slowly, but he ended the season with a .296 batting average. The Dodgers, however, placed third in their league, which was a disappointment.

In spite of their subpar season on the field, the Dodgers continued to make news. They signed Roy Campanella in 1948 and then Don Newcombe in 1949. Jackie Robinson had paved the way for them. In the meantime, Larry Doby became the first black player on an American League team roster. He joined the Cleveland Indians in July 1947 and went on to be named an All-Star for the years 1949 through 1955.

Aside from baseball, big changes occurred in Robinson's personal life. He and Rachel had a son, Jackie Jr., in 1946, and in 1947 they moved from their room in the McAlpin Hotel in Manhattan to a larger apartment in Brooklyn.

Shortly after Robinson broke the color line, Larry Doby (right) became the first African-American to play in the American League.

Jackie and Jackie Jr. in 1949

Looking Back at His Rookie Season

At the close of the 1947 season, much had changed for Robinson and for the game of baseball. He recalled his feelings about the year.

I had started the season as a lonely man. . . . I ended it feeling like a member of a solid team. The Dodgers were a championship team because all of us had learned something. I had learned how to exercise self-control—to answer insults, violence, and injustice with silence—and I had learned how to earn the respect of my teammates. They had learned that it's not skin color but talent and ability that [count]. Maybe even the bigots had learned that, too.

"Did You See Jackie Hit That Ball?"

Many singers and songwriters honored Jackie Robinson by recording songs about him. Some of these included "The Jackie Robinson Boogie" and "Jackie Robinson Blues." Probably the most famous was Buddy Johnson's 1949 hit entitled "Did You See Jackie Hit That Ball?" It went like this:

Did you see Jackie hit that ball?
It went zoom across the left field wall.
Yeah boy, yes, yes. Jackie hit that ball.

And when he swung that bat,
The crowd went wild,
Because he knocked that ball a solid mile.
Yeah boy, yes, yes. Jackie hit that ball.

Satchel [Paige] is mellow,
So is Campanella.
Newcombe and Doby, too.
But it's a natural fact,
When Jackie comes to bat,
The other team is through.

Did you see Jackie Robinson hit that ball?
Did he hit it boy, and that ain't all.
He stole home.
Yes, yes, Jackie's real gone.

SPEAKING HIS MIND

After two years of turning the other cheek, Robinson was finally given permission from Branch Rickey to speak his mind. Rickey felt that Robinson had been silent long enough, and they had accomplished their initial goals. So in 1949, the world heard what the brilliant player really thought. He spoke freely at press conferences and was quick to give his opinions on all sorts of matters. He talked about racism in baseball as well as on the streets of the United States.

That same year, Jackie Robinson appeared before the House Un-American Activities Committee (HUAC) in Washington, D.C. This committee sought to expose **Communists** living within the United States. It interviewed numerous people in an attempt to test their loyalty and convince them to name acquaintances suspected of having Communist ties. In the end, the committee overstepped its bounds and ruined the lives of many U.S. citizens.

HUAC's members were outraged by statements American singer and actor Paul Robeson had made. Robeson was upset by the rampant racism of the United States, so he explained that if war were to break out between the United States and the

Soviet Union, he saw no reason why black Americans should fight. In his opinion, black Americans were not treated fairly and thus should feel no loyalty to their own country.

HUAC asked Jackie Robinson to address this issue. In his statement before the committee, he admitted that he knew little about Communism, but he understood Robeson's anger with the racism he endured in the United States. Robinson said that while he felt a strong loyalty to his country, he would continue to fight for equal rights for all of its citizens.

Performer Paul Robeson made some statements about racism in the United States that angered the House Un-American Activities Committee.

MVP AND MOVIE STAR

The 1949 season was a great one for Robinson. His batting average (.342) and number of bases stolen (37) were the highest in the league. That year, he was named the National League Most Valuable Player, and he signed a new contract for $35,000 a year. The Dodgers again won the pennant, but they lost the World Series to the New York Yankees.

The following year, the Robinsons added a daughter, Sharon, to their family, and before the season started Jackie headed to Hollywood. There he starred as himself in *The Jackie Robinson Story*, a movie about his life. Though the film received mixed reviews, Robinson had fun in the role.

HIGHS AND LOWS

During the seasons that followed, Jackie Robinson's life was marked with highs and lows. The Dodgers experienced exciting victories but also endured tough losses. Robinson gained more and more acceptance from the fans in many cities, but in some places fans still chanted racial insults at him. At one 1950 game in Cincinnati, Robinson even received a death threat, but he appreciated the support he got from his teammates—outfielder Gene Hermanski even joked that they should all wear number 42, as a way to confuse the alleged shooter—and nothing came of the threat after all.

One great loss for Robinson was Branch Rickey's resignation as president of the Dodgers. He was replaced by Walter O'Malley, a man who was not fond of the outspoken Robinson.

The Robinson family, shown here in 1962, at their Stamford, Connecticut, home

At one point, Robinson was quick to criticize the New York Yankees, who still did not have a black man on their team, and he was always eager to discuss the general lack of rights for African-Americans in the United States. Many people sympathized with all that Robinson had lived through, while others felt he should just play baseball and be grateful for what he had.

In 1950, the Robinsons moved to St. Albans, a New York City suburb, and two years later, they welcomed another son, David, to their family. Then they began looking for an even larger home, but they faced difficulty when looking in all-white neighborhoods. Sellers raised their prices when they heard that a black family was interested in buying, or homes were suddenly pulled off the market altogether. Robinson may have broken the color line in baseball, but U.S. society in general hadn't been affected very much. Eventually, in 1955, the Robinsons moved to Stamford, Connecticut, where they were among the few African-Americans in the predominantly white community. At times, the children felt uncomfortable there, but Robinson knew that only courage could bring about change. He remained in Stamford for the rest of his life.

Robinson experienced the streaks and the slumps that most baseball players do. On the baseball diamond, he performed well in some seasons and not so well in others, but overall his performance was excellent. His lifetime batting average was .311, but during the years between 1949 and 1953, he hit .329, drove in 463 runs, stole 155 bases, and scored 540 times. It wasn't just that his stats were impressive either; he brought an energy and enthusiasm to the baseball field that was felt by both the fans and his teammates.

Though 1955 was not one of his best years, it was a year to remember. The Dodgers won the pennant and once again faced the New York Yankees in the World Series. Robinson was getting older by then and—unknown to his teammates—he had been diagnosed with diabetes, so his play was not at its best. In spite of his physical limitations, he gave his fans a moment to remember in game one of the series. In the eighth inning, the Yankees were ahead 6–4; there were two outs, and Robinson was at third base. He watched the

Robinson shocked Yankee catcher Yogi Berra and pumped up his teammates by stealing home in game one of the 1955 World Series.

pitcher's timing, and he studied the actions of legendary catcher Yogi Berra. Then, after a given pitch, he suddenly jumped off third base and barreled down the line. Surprised by such an action, the pitcher quickly threw the ball back to Berra but not in time— Robinson had stolen home. This gutsy move in the opening game fired up the Dodgers, who lost that game but went on to win the series. At last, Jackie Robinson was a member of a world championship team.

CHAPTER 6

AFTER BASEBALL

Robinson clearing out his locker after leaving the Brooklyn Dodgers

As Jackie Robinson reached his late thirties, he began to realize that he couldn't play baseball forever. He thought about his options and wondered what the future might hold for him. Many baseball players, as they approach retirement from the game, become team managers or they take administrative positions in the teams' organizations. In 1957, however, these were not options for an African-American player.

Closed Doors

In *Great Time Coming*, biographer David Faulkner explained Robinson's position at the end of his baseball career:

In these final seasons, Robinson became once again a man searching for his place. He let it be known—to Branch Rickey and to others close to him—that for the barriers to fall completely, those to the coaching lines, the dugout, and the front office must fall as well. Robinson did not seriously consider whether he wanted to stay in baseball, because he knew those doors were still tightly closed. He was given no encouragement.

CALLING IT QUITS

During the 1956 season, Jackie Robinson was approached by executives at Chock Full O'Nuts, a restaurant chain in New York City. William Black, the company president, offered Robinson a position as vice president of community affairs.

Robinson had always been interested in business, and he saw this offer as an important opportunity. In the meantime, the Dodgers announced they would be leaving Ebbets Field and moving to Los Angeles, a decision that broke the hearts of the people of Brooklyn. At the end of that year, the Dodgers also traded Robinson to the New York Giants, but the now-veteran player knew it was time to call it quits. In January 1957, Jackie Robinson retired from baseball.

IN THE COMMUNITY

Robinson took his position at Chock Full O'Nuts very seriously, and he worked hard in his role. It was his job to improve the company's reputation as well as strengthen its name in the community. Through this role, he developed a better understanding of big business and its impact on politics and government.

Spending time with fellow Chock Full O'Nuts employees

One organization he supported was the NAACP. This group fought for civil rights, and Robinson raised funds for them and appeared at many of their rallies.

Aside from his business responsibilities, Robinson worked to support the NAACP and the fight for civil rights.

Robinson with Richard Nixon (above) and Martin Luther King, Jr. (below)

During this time, Robinson also became involved in politics. Prior to the 1960 presidential election, he met with both candidates—John F. Kennedy, the Democrat, and Richard Nixon, the Republican. Traditionally, Democrats have been perceived as more liberal and more committed to civil rights than Republicans are, but Robinson was more impressed with Nixon than with Kennedy. He threw his support behind the Republican, which may seem like an odd move. At that time though, many black voters, including Martin Luther King Jr., were having a hard time deciding which candidate would best serve African-American interests. Kennedy went on to become president, and he shared a strained relationship with Robinson. Years later, when Robinson saw the support Kennedy gave to Dr. King and to civil rights in general, Robinson admitted he had made an error in judgment.

In the years to come, Jackie Robinson worked closely with Martin Luther King Jr. and other civil rights leaders. He wanted to make a difference and to improve the lives of black Americans, but ultimately, he found that change was often a slow and frustrating process.

THE HALL OF FAME

In 1962, Jackie Robinson was eligible for the Baseball Hall of Fame because he had been retired from the game for five years. To reach the Hall of Fame is the highest honor in baseball, but Robinson did not have high hopes. Being named to the Hall is the result of voting by the Baseball Writers' Association of America, and Robinson knew that many of these reporters resented his outspoken temperament. However, the writers did elect him that year, and he was both surprised and overwhelmed by the honor. He traveled to Cooperstown, New York, where the Hall of Fame is located, for his induction.

There he thanked his family and his fans, as well as his team and Branch Rickey, for all their years of support.

MORE POLITICS AND ANOTHER SUCCESS

In 1964, Jackie Robinson resigned from Chock Full O'Nuts and joined Nelson Rockefeller's campaign. Rockefeller was the governor of New York and hoped to win the Republican nomination for president. Robinson believed in Rockefeller, a liberal Republican, and thought he could improve employment conditions for black Americans. He worked hard as Rockefeller's special assistant, but in the end the Republicans nominated Barry Goldwater, who was defeated by Lyndon Johnson in the election for president that year. Robinson was very disappointed with the failure of the Rockefeller campaign, but he tried to find other areas in which he could make a difference.

After finishing his work with Rockefeller, Robinson focused his energy on helping to start the Freedom National Bank. This bank—owned and operated by African-Americans and based in Harlem—offered loans and financial support to black businesses in the community. Robinson raised money to start the bank and then served on its board of directors. The Freedom National Bank helped strengthen many Harlem businesses, and it proved to be a great success.

Martin Luther King Jr.

Jackie Robinson was deeply influenced by Martin Luther King Jr., and he respected all that this courageous activist did with his life. When King was killed in 1968, Robinson remembered:

At the funeral services, I was plunged into deep contemplation as I thought of the sadness of saying farewell to a man who died still clinging to a dream of integration and peace and nonviolence. I could only hope that perhaps his death was symbolically hopeful. Perhaps after the streets of American cities were no longer haunted by angry blacks seeking to avenge the assassination, we would find ourselves. Perhaps Dr. Martin Luther King's last full measure of devotion for the cause of brotherhood would not prove to have been in vain.

Jackie Robinson supported Nelson Rockefeller (left) in his campaign to win the Republican presidential nomination in 1964.

CHAPTER 7

REMEMBERING A REMARKABLE MAN

The remaining years of Jackie Robinson's life were marked by tragedy and illness. In 1965, Branch Rickey died, and in many ways Robinson felt as though he had lost a father. Rickey had risked so much and had challenged Robinson to be a better man as well as a better baseball player. Robinson was overcome with grief. Robinson's mother died three years later, and he mourned the loss of this constant source of love and support.

A Letter to Branch Rickey

In 1950, Jackie Robinson was sad to see Branch Rickey leave the Brooklyn Dodgers organization. What follows is an excerpt from a letter Robinson wrote to Rickey at that time:

It is certainly tough on everyone in Brooklyn to have you leave the organization but to me it's much worse and I don't mind saying we (my family) hate to see you go but realize that baseball is like that and anything can happen. It has been the finest experience I have had being associated with you and I want to thank you very much for all you have meant not only to me and my family but to the entire country and particularly the members of our race. I am glad for your sake that I had a small part to do with the success of your efforts and must admit it was your constant guidance that enabled me to do it. Regardless of what happens to me in the future it all can be placed on what you have done and believe me I appreciate it.

LOSING JACKIE JR.

In 1971, Robinson was dealt another terrible blow, this time involving the life of his older son. Jackie Jr. had always been a bit of a handful, and he had been in trouble throughout his youth. In 1965, Jackie Jr. was wounded in action while serving in the Vietnam War (1950s–1975). He briefly returned to duty but was discharged in 1967. He returned home, angry and confused, and quickly developed a problem with drug abuse.

At one point, the young man was arrested and given the choice of jail or a **drug rehabilitation** program. He chose the latter, and he worked hard to overcome his addiction. After finishing the program, Jackie Jr. went on to become a counselor and help other drug addicts. Sadly, just as he was getting his life back on track, he was killed in a car accident. Jackie and Rachel Robinson were devastated.

THE END OF AN OUTSTANDING LIFE

In the early 1970s, Jackie Robinson's health began to decline. He continued to suffer from diabetes and had developed heart disease as well. He walked with a limp, and his eyesight was very poor.

In June 1972, despite his poor health, Robinson made a very important

opposite: Robinson was always close to his mother, Mallie, so her death in 1956 was very hard on him.

Throughout his career, Robinson brought courage and excellence to the game of baseball.

Rachel Robinson created the Jackie Robinson Foundation after her husband's death.

public appearance at Dodger Stadium in Los Angeles. He attended a ceremony to mark the twenty-fifth anniversary of his major league debut. That day his famous number 42 was retired from the Dodger lineup.

A few months later, on October 24, Robinson died in Stamford, Connecticut. His death was a quiet one, an ironic end to a life full of energy, accomplishment, and controversy. His courage on the baseball diamond led the way for other black athletes to compete in a variety of sports. Boxing legend Joe Louis once praised him by saying, "Jackie is my hero. He don't bite his tongue for nothing. I just don't have the guts, you might call it, to say what he says. And don't talk as good either, that's for sure. But he talks the way he feels."

Thousands of people turned out for Robinson's funeral, and among those who spoke about him was thirty-one-year-old minister Jesse Jackson. The year following his death, Rachel Robinson created the Jackie Robinson Foundation. This nonprofit group helps support minority youths and provides college scholarships to those in need. The foundation is a fitting legacy to Jackie Robinson and his goal of improving social justice.

Fifty Years Later

In 1997, baseball celebrated the fiftieth anniversary of Jackie Robinson's breaking the color line. At a game between the New York Mets and the Los Angeles Dodgers at New York's Shea Stadium on April 15, Robinson's number 42 was retired from all of baseball. President Bill Clinton attended the ceremony, and below is part of what he had to say:

It is hard to believe that 50 years ago at Ebbets Field a 28-year-old rookie changed the face of baseball forever and the face of America forever....

Today I think we should remember that Jackie Robinson's legacy did not end with baseball, for afterward he spent the rest of his life trying to open doors and keep them open for all kinds of people. He knew that education, not sports, was the key to success in life for nearly everyone. And he took that message to young people wherever he went.

I can't help thinking that if Jackie Robinson were here with us tonight, he would say that we have done a lot of good in the last 50 years, but we can do better. We have achieved equality on the playing field, but we need to establish equality in the boardrooms of baseball, and throughout corporate America....

And he would remind us—look around this stadium tonight—that as we sit side by side at baseball games, we must make sure that we walk out of these stadiums together. We must stand for something more magnificent even than a grand slam home run. We ought to have a grand slam society, a good society where all of us have a chance to work together for a better tomorrow for our children. Let that be the true legacy of Jackie Robinson's wonderful, remarkable career and life.

TIMELINE

1919	Jack Roosevelt Robinson is born on January 31 in Cairo, Georgia
1920	Moves with his mother and siblings to Pasadena, California
1937	Begins college at Pasadena Junior College
1939	Transfers to UCLA and letters in four sports
1942	Joins the U.S. Army and fights for the right to go to Officers' Candidate School
1944	Stands trial for refusing to sit in the back of an army bus; is discharged from the army
1945	Plays Negro League baseball as a Kansas City Monarch; meets with Branch Rickey in August and signs a contract to play for the Montreal Royals
1946	Marries Rachel Isum; plays for the Montreal Royals
1947	On April 15, plays first game for the Brooklyn Dodgers; is named Rookie of the Year for the National League
1949	Testifies before the House Un-American Activities Committee; is named Most Valuable Player in the National League
1950	Stars in *The Jackie Robinson Story*
1955	Dodgers defeat the New York Yankees to win the World Series
1956	Dodgers move to Los Angeles; Robinson is traded to the New York Giants
1957	Robinson retires from baseball; takes position as a vice president for Chock Full O'Nuts
1960	Campaigns for presidential candidate Richard Nixon
1962	Is inducted into the Baseball Hall of Fame
1964	Serves in Nelson Rockefeller's campaign; helps found the Freedom National Bank
1972	Dies on October 24 in Stamford, Connecticut

GLOSSARY

athletic eligibility: a term during which an athlete is allowed to play sports during high school and college

bigotry: a strong dislike of certain groups of people, usually racially motivated

civil rights: equal rights and freedoms for all citizens

Communists: people who support communism, a political system in which all property is owned by the government

court-martial: a trial for members of the armed forces

debut: a first public appearance

Deep South: the southeastern region of the United States

discrimination: unjust treatment of people based on race, background, or religion

drug rehabilitation: a program that helps drug addicts overcome their problems and regain good health

exhibition games: games played between teams just as a show for the public; these games do not count in the regular season

farm team: a minor-league team, usually affiliated with a major-league team for the purpose of developing younger players

integrated: composed of all groups of people no matter what their race or background

Jim Crow laws: laws that discriminated against African-American citizens

juvenile delinquent: a young person in trouble with the law

major league baseball: North American professional baseball played in the National League and the American League

minstrel: relating to the performance of song and dance often by traveling musicians

pennant: the championship title of a baseball league; in the major leagues, the winners of the individual pennants face each other in the World Series

petition: a letter requesting a change in policy and signed by many people

racists: those who believe that one race is superior to all others and judge others on the basis of their race

rookie: a professional athlete in his or her first year

scout: a person sent to observe athletes and report on their ability

segregation: the separation of groups of people, usually based on race, background, or religion

sharecropper: a farmer who works a section of land in return for part of the profits

slurs: insulting remarks

vandalized: damaged, usually on purpose

vaudeville: stage entertainment that includes acrobats, singers, dancers, and comedians

TO FIND OUT MORE

BOOKS

Bergman, Irwin B. *Jackie Robinson.* (Junior World Biographies) Broomall, Penn.: Chelsea House, 1994.

Brashler, William. *The Story of Negro League Baseball.* New York: Ticknor & Fields, 1994.

Deangelis, Gina. *Jackie Robinson.* (Overcoming Adversity) Broomall, Penn.: Chelsea House, 2000.

Dunn, Herb. *Jackie Robinson: Young Sports Trailblazer.* New York: Aladdin, 1999.

Rudeen, Kenneth. *Jackie Robinson.* (Trophy Chapter Books) New York: HarperTrophy, 1996.

Santella, Andrew. *Jackie Robinson Breaks the Color Line.* (Cornerstones of Freedom) Danbury, Conn.: Children's Press, 1996.

INTERNET SITES

By Popular Demand: Jackie Robinson and Other Baseball Highlights
http://www.memory.loc.gov/ammem/jrhtml/jrhome/html
A site sponsored by the Library of Congress and chronicling Robinson's life and accomplishments.

Jackie Robinson: Civil Rights Advocate
http://www.nara.gov/education/teaching/robinson/robmain.html
A site sponsored by the National Archives and Records Administration; includes letters Robinson wrote as well as a number of quotations.

The Jackie Robinson Foundation
http://www.jackierobinson.org
To learn more about the charity founded in Jackie Robinson's name; also includes biographical information.

The National Baseball Hall of Fame
http://www.baseballhalloffame.org/index.htm
To learn about the Hall of Fame and all of its honorees.

INDEX

INDEX *(continued)*

About the Author

Lucia Raatma received her bachelor's degree in English literature from the University of South Carolina and her master's degree in cinema studies from New York University. She has written a wide range of books for young people. When she is not researching or writing, she enjoys going to movies, playing tennis, practicing yoga, and spending time with her husband, daughter, and golden retriever. She lives in New York.